Mae the Panda Fairy

For Lara, with love

Special thanks to Rachel Elliot

No part of this work may be reproduced, stored in a retrieval system, or transmitted in any form or by any means, electronic, mechanical, photocopying, recording, or otherwise, without written permission of the publisher. For information regarding permission, write to Rainbow Magic Limited c/o HIT Entertainment, 830 South Greenville Avenue, Allen, TX 75002-3320.

ISBN 978-0-545-70844-9

All rights reserved. Published by Scholastic Inc., 557 Broadway, New York, NY 10012, by arrangement with Rainbow Magic Limited.

SCHOLASTIC and associated logos are trademarks and/or registered trademarks of Scholastic Inc. RAINBOW MAGIC is a trademark of Rainbow Magic Limited. Reg. U.S. Patent & Trademark Office and other countries. HIT and the HIT logo are trademarks of HIT Entertainment Limited.

12 11 10 9 8 7 6 5 4   17 18 19/0

Printed in the U.S.A.   40

First Scholastic printing, January 2015

Mae the Panda Fairy

by Daisy Meadows

SCHOLASTIC INC.

The Fairyland Palace

Meadow

Stream

Beehive

Arctic Tundra

Eucalyptus Forest

Tropical Waterfall

Wild Woods
Nature
Reserve

Jack Frost's
Ice Castle

To Jack Frost's Zoo

Watering Hole

Pagoda

Desert Oasis

I love animals—yes, I do,
I want my very own private zoo!
I'll capture all the animals one by one,
With fairy magic to help me get it done!

A koala, a tiger, an Arctic fox,
I'll keep them in cages with giant locks.
Every kind of animal will be there,
A panda, a meerkat, a honey bear.
The animals will be my property,
I'll be master of my own menagerie!

Contents

A Visitor from Fairyland

Kirsty Tate gazed happily at the rows of bushes, her bare arm resting on the open window as the car traveled along the bumpy country road. Pretty red, yellow, and pink flowers were tangled among the green leaves. She could smell the tangy aroma of cut grass and the earthiness of freshly turned soil.

"We're almost there, girls," said Mrs. Tate from the driver's seat. "Look!"

She slowed the car and pointed at a sign at the side of the winding road.

2 MILES—WILD WOODS NATURE RESERVE

Kirsty smiled at her best friend, Rachel Walker, who was sitting beside her.

"I'm so excited," said Rachel. "The sun's shining, we've got the whole summer vacation stretched out ahead of us, and a whole week to spend here at the reserve with the animals."

It was the start of summer vacation, and Kirsty and Rachel were on their way to Wild Woods, their local nature reserve. Rachel was staying with Kirsty, and their parents had arranged for them to spend every day that week at the reserve as volunteers. As the car turned up a rough, narrow road, their hearts raced with anticipation.

"I can't wait to help out as a junior ranger," said Kirsty.

"It will be so cool to see the animals!"

At the end of the road was an archway, printed with green words:

WELCOME TO WILD WOODS
NATURE RESERVE

Mrs. Tate drove through the archway and stopped the car next to a small wooden hut. The door of the hut opened and a tan woman with dark brown hair came out. She was wearing khaki shorts, a white shirt, and hiking boots. She waved at them and smiled.

"Look, there's Becky," said Mrs. Tate. "She's the head of Wild Woods."

Rachel and Kirsty jumped out of the car, and Becky walked over to them.

"It's great to see you," said Becky, shaking their hands. "I'm really glad that you'll be spending the week with us. It's great to meet young people who are interested in conservation."

"We can't wait to get started!" said Rachel excitedly.

"I thought you could begin by exploring the reserve on your own a little," said Becky. "It's the best way to get a feel for it. I'll meet you back here this afternoon and give you your first task."

"That sounds great!" Kirsty cheered.

"A real adventure!" Rachel added.

"These two love adventures!" said Mrs. Tate with a laugh.

The girls exchanged a secret, happy glance. Kirsty's mother had no idea how many adventures they had already had! They were friends with all the Rainbow Magic fairies, and had often visited

Fairyland and helped foil Jack Frost's evil plans.

They grabbed their backpacks and some supplies for the day.

"Do you have everything?" asked Mrs. Tate kindly.

Kirsty peered into her backpack. "Camera, notebook, raincoat, pens, binoculars, sunscreen . . ." She grinned at her mother. "Yes, I think I've remembered everything!"

Mrs. Tate kissed her and gave Kirsty a hug. "Have a fantastic time," she said.

Rachel and Kirsty waved good-bye and hurried down a winding path into the reserve. As soon as they were out of sight, Kirsty paused and took a deep breath of fresh air. "I feel as if there's no one else for miles and miles," she said.

"It's wonderful!" Rachel smiled, turning around slowly on the spot. "I can see dragonflies, bumblebees, and even a kingfisher!"

They were standing beside a large
pond, which was surrounded by
catttails. Everywhere they looked, they
saw animals. Hares peeked at them,
ducks paddled nearby, and otters
slipped into the water. Kirsty fumbled

in her backpack and pulled out her camera.

"This place is incredible," she said, taking picture after picture.

"Look over there," said Rachel, pulling out her camera, too. "The frog on that lily pad looks just like my stuffed animal at home."

"He does look familiar," Kirsty agreed, looking through her camera lens and zooming in. "Hang on— that's no ordinary frog! It's Bertram!"

Their friend, a royal frog footman from Fairyland, waved and came hopping over to them.

Rachel and Kirsty knelt down beside the edge of the pond and smiled at him.

"Hello, Rachel and Kirsty!" he said in a surprised voice. "I didn't expect to meet you two here!"

"We didn't expect to see you, either," said Rachel with a giggle.

"I have relatives in the human world," Bertram explained. "I just visited them."

"We're here helping out at the nature

reserve," Kirsty explained. "We're taking a little tour."

"Yes, this is a very nice nature reserve," said Bertram. "Not as good as the one in Fairyland, of course."

"I didn't know there was a nature reserve in Fairyland," said Rachel.

"Oh, yes. It's wonderful there," said Bertram. "Would you like to visit?"

"Yes, please!" said Rachel.

"We'd love to!" Kirsty exclaimed. "But how can we get there without fairy magic?"

"Should we use our lockets?" asked Rachel. "They still have a little bit of fairy dust inside them."

"There's no need for that," said Bertram with a smile. "I have a little magic of my own!"

Animal
Thief!

There was a far-off sound like leaves
rustling in the wind, and then a silvery
starburst surrounded them. The girls felt
wings growing on their backs as they
shrank to fairy-size. When the sparkles
cleared, they were standing in a magical,
green clearing next to Bertram.

They heard a squeak of surprise and saw their old friend Fluffy the squirrel staring at them in astonishment.

"Rachel! Kirsty!" he exclaimed. "Welcome to the Fairyland Nature Reserve! I didn't know you were visiting Fairyland today."

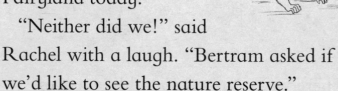

"Neither did we!" said Rachel with a laugh. "Bertram asked if we'd like to see the nature reserve."

"You're always welcome here," said Fluffy. "Follow me and I'll give you a guided tour."

The girls said good-bye to Bertram and then set off after Fluffy. He scampered down a winding path. Moments later,

they were flying through a snowy
Antarctic scene, surrounded by penguins.
Kirsty and Rachel still had their cameras
around their necks, and they snapped
photo after photo of the playful black-
and-white animals.

Around the next corner was a jungle habitat. Fluffy leaped through the high trees, calling out to the mischievous monkeys who were swinging from the branches. *Click! Click! Click!* Rachel's and Kirsty's cameras were filling up with photos.

"I wonder if these photos will come out all right when the cameras return to human-size," said Kirsty.

"If they do, let's promise to keep them a secret," said Rachel.

Fluffy paused to talk to a red-and-gold parrot, and the girls landed on a branch and linked their little fingers in a special best friends' promise. Then they shared a happy smile. They hadn't expected their nature reserve trip to be this exciting!

Fluffy scampered down a tree and into a spring meadow, filled with buttercups and daisies. Rachel and Kirsty followed.

"It's wonderful how we can travel from one habitat to another so quickly," said Kirsty happily.

On the far side of the meadow was a fluttering cloud of butterflies. Rachel pointed at them in delight and lifted her camera to take a picture.

"They're coming this way," she said.

"Hang on," said Kirsty. "They're much too big to be butterflies. They're fairies!"

The girls started waving, and the seven pretty fairies flew toward them, smiling with excitement.

"You're Rachel and Kirsty, aren't you?" asked a dark-haired fairy with a pretty patterned top. "We weren't expecting such important visitors today! We're the Baby Animal Rescue Fairies, and we look after all the baby animals in the Fairyland Nature Reserve. I'm Kimberly the Koala Fairy."

"It's so nice to meet you," said Rachel with a bright smile.

The other fairies introduced themselves as Kitty the Tiger Fairy, Mara the Meerkat Fairy, Savannah the Zebra Fairy, Mae the Panda Fairy, Rosie the Honey Bear Fairy, and Nora the Arctic Fox Fairy. The girls noticed that each fairy had an animal key chain clipped to her clothes, to match the animal she looked after.

"I hope you don't mind us taking a few photos," said Kirsty.

"Of course not," said Kimberly. "I hope you get some good pictures. All the animals are friendly, as long as you don't get too close or startle them."

Suddenly, there was a gigantic roar and the ground started to shake. The fairies clutched at one another in fear.

"What is it?" cried Nora.

"An earthquake!" Savannah exclaimed.

They saw Bertram hopping toward them, shouting and waving. The noise grew even louder. All around the meadow, birds flew into the air, petrified. Terrified woodland animals raced back and forth in the grass, not knowing which direction to choose. The girls turned around and gasped. An enormous ice-blue monster truck was hurtling toward them at a fast speed!

The truck screeched to a halt inches from where they were standing. When the engine was turned off, the roar died down. Then Jack Frost opened the door and jumped out, followed by several goblins. Bertram arrived beside the girls, looking very angry.

"Your truck scared all the animals!" he cried.

"Don't be silly," snapped Jack Frost. "I *love* animals! That's why I'm here! I want one of every kind of animal in the world in my own private zoo."

"But that's wrong," said Rachel. "Animals are living creatures. You shouldn't just collect them."

"Whatever!" Jack Frost hissed. "It's none of your business."

"No, it definitely *is* our business," said

Mara, stepping forward. "We're the Baby Animal Rescue Fairies. If you won't listen to our friends, maybe you'll listen to us."

"Fat chance!" cackled one of the goblins standing behind Jack Frost.

"Nanny nanny boo-boo, stinks to be you," said another goblin rudely, putting his thumb to his nose and wagging his fingers.

Jack Frost just curled his lip and lifted his wand.

"You'll never stop
my selfish joys!
You silly fairies,
I'll take your toys!"

He waved his wand and there was a blinding bolt of ice-blue magic. In a flash, Jack Frost was holding all seven of the fairies' animal key chains!

Lost!

The fairies cried out and Jack Frost laughed, throwing the key chains into the air and juggling them like toys.

"Give those back!" Rachel demanded.

"What, these?" asked Jack Frost, holding them out to her.

Rachel reached out to take them, but he snatched them away, cackling with laughter. He threw them to his goblins, who dropped them all.

"BUTTERFINGERS!" Jack Frost roared. "Pick them up NOW, and round up every animal in this silly nature reserve. I'll take them all!"

"Yes sir, right away, sir!" babbled the goblins, gathering the key chains in their arms.

"We have to stop them!" Kirsty exclaimed, looking worried.

Fluffy raced forward and squeaked at

the goblins as loudly as he could. The cowardly goblins screamed and ran away, still clutching the key chains. Jack Frost watched them disappear among the distant trees, and shook his fist after them. Then he turned to face the fairies. His eyes narrowed to mean slits.

"Fine," he said. "FINE! If I can't have these Fairyland animals, I'll just take animals from the human world instead!"

He jumped back into his truck and it roared to life. A huge cloud of blue smoke puffed into the fairies' faces. Then the truck zoomed away and disappeared from sight.

"What are we going to do?" asked
Rosie. "Without our magic key chains,
we can't protect the animals in the
human world!"

Kitty turned to Rachel and Kirsty with
tears in her eyes.

"We have to stop him and save the
animals," she said. "But how?"

"We'll help," said Rachel at once.

"We'll do everything we can," said
Kirsty. "I don't know where we're going
to start, though."

Mae the Panda Fairy threw her arms
around the girls.
"Thank you so
much," she said.
"The other
fairies have
told us how kind

you are. And I think I have an idea that might help."

She whispered something to the six other Baby Animal Rescue Fairies, and then they all lifted their wands together and waved them in unison. Colored fairy dust swirled from the tips of their wands and spun together in the air, forming a small sparkling cloud. It moved over the heads of Rachel and Kirsty, and then sprinkled down on them.

Instantly, the noises around them seemed to change. The air had been full of the squawks of birds, but now the squawks sounded more like voices. Adding to the noise, there were soft, squeaky voices from below their feet.

"Where's my nest? I've lost my nest!"

"Whose feet are these?"

"What's that? Is it food?"

"Who said that?" asked Rachel in amazement.

The fairies laughed.

"We just gave you the ability to communicate with animals," said Mae. "It should help you find our magic key chains."

Rachel and Kirsty shared a thrilled smile, holding hands. They slid their cameras into their backpacks.

"I want to visit my panda friends in the human world," said Mae. "I need to warn them that Jack Frost might be coming. Will you come with me?"

Rachel and Kirsty nodded eagerly, and Mae lifted her wand above her head.

"Let Rachel and Kirsty come and see where pandas wander wild and free."

Instantly, the meadow around the girls vanished. They were standing beside a beautiful pagoda at the top of a mountain, and they were human-size again. A dense forest of bamboo covered the mountain. Mae fluttered next to them, looking around in delight. It was obvious that she loved this place.

Even though it was warm, it was also raining. The girls pulled their raincoats out of their backpacks and put them on. Mae tucked herself inside Rachel's hood.

"Come on, let's go," she said. "Keep an eye out for the pandas!"

They pushed their way between the tall bamboo stems, and raindrops pattered down on their hoods.

They hadn't gone very far before Kirsty heard a rustling sound. She reached out her hand and held Rachel's arm.

"Listen!" she whispered.

Rachel suddenly felt as if it were Christmas Eve and Santa was on his way. Could they really be about to see a real-life panda in the wild? They crept toward the sound, treading as softly as they could. Then they heard a soft voice calling through the forest.

"Pan Pan, where are you?"

"Who's that?" Rachel asked Mae in a low voice.

The soft voice was sad and urgent. "Come back to Mama," it said.

Then Kirsty spotted a giant panda in a tree above them. "We can understand animals now," she said. "Remember the fairies' spell?"

"Of course!" said Rachel. "Wow!"

Kirsty waved at the beautiful panda.

"Hello," she called. "I'm Kirsty, and

this is my friend
Rachel."

The giant panda's eyes
widened, but she didn't
reply. She just stared down
at them, looking confused
and scared.

Mae flew out of Rachel's hood
and zoomed up to hover beside the giant
panda. The girls couldn't hear what she
was saying, but after a long pause, the
panda began to climb down the tree. She
moved quickly and gracefully. When
she reached the ground, she turned and
sat down beside the girls.

"I'm sorry I didn't answer you at first,"
she said. "I didn't know if I could trust
you. My baby, my little Pan Pan, has
disappeared!"

The Bamboo Forest

"I'm so sorry," said Rachel, putting her hand on the mother panda's paw. "Will you tell us about it? We might be able to help you."

"Pan Pan is only seven months old," she said. "He's just started eating bamboo, so I went to find him some extra-juicy shoots. When I came back, he was gone!"

Rachel and Kirsty exchanged a suspicious glance.

"Do you think that the goblins might have taken Pan Pan for Jack Frost?" asked Kirsty.

"We need to have a good look at the place where you last saw Pan Pan," said Rachel to the mother panda. "Can you take us there?"

She led them deeper into the bamboo forest, until they reached a big clearing. "This is where I last saw Pan Pan," she said sadly.

Rachel and Kirsty looked around, and then Rachel shouted.

"Over there. Look!" she cried.

They could see huge footprints in the mud. Whoever had made them had large, flat feet and long, spread-out toes.

"Goblins!" said Kirsty. "I knew it! I bet that if we follow these footprints, we'll find Pan Pan."

"It'll be easier to follow them if we can all fly," said Mae. She flicked her wand, and there was a small explosion of silver fairy dust that made the mother panda jump. The silver sparkles swirled around the two girls. As they shrank to fairy-size, they felt their wings growing on their backs.

"We'll be back as soon as we have news of Pan Pan," Kirsty promised the mother panda.

The three fairies rose into the air and waved good-bye. Then they followed the huge footprints away from the clearing and through the forest of bamboo.

"Bamboo trees are amazingly tall," said Rachel. "I didn't know they could grow so high."

"Bamboo is one of the fastest-growing plants in the world," Mae told them in a proud voice. "It makes a wonderful food for pandas."

"I hope it stays like this forever," said Kirsty to Mae.

They hadn't been following the footprints for very long before they heard a lot of shrieking and squabbling.

"That sounds like goblins," said Rachel. "Come on!"

The rain had slowed, so the girls put away their raincoats in order to fly faster. They zigzagged through the trees and bamboo stems until they reached a babbling mountain stream. There, on the bank, were four noisy goblins!

Three of the goblins seemed to be trying to push one another into the water. The fourth goblin, who had very large ears, was sitting on a log, cuddling something black and white in his arms.

"It's Pan Pan!" cried Mae.

The fairies fluttered closer and hid behind some bamboo leaves. The goblin was tickling Pan Pan with a little fluffy toy, and the panda was chuckling.

"Mae, that's your magic key chain, isn't it?" asked Kirsty in excitement.

Mae nodded eagerly. "You're right. Oh, girls, we've found the baby panda

and my key chain. But how can we get them both back from the goblin?"

Just then, the three goblins who had been wrestling on the bank turned to the goblin with big ears.

"We've been messing around here long enough," said the tallest goblin. "Stop cuddling that panda. We have to get it to the Ice Castle, so it can be the first animal in Jack Frost's zoo."

"Not IT . . . HE!" shouted the big-eared goblin. "Anyway, we can't go yet. He's very thirsty!"

The other three goblins rolled their eyes as he stood up and took Pan Pan over to the clear stream. He put the little panda down to have a few sips of water. When Pan Pan had had enough, he sat back and looked around. The big-eared goblin held out the magic key chain, and Pan Pan scampered back to him and snuggled up in his lap.

"Finally," said the tallest goblin. "Now let's go."

"We can't go just yet," said the big-eared goblin. "He's taking a nap."

The other goblins groaned and Kirsty turned to Mae with a frown.

"Why does Pan Pan like the goblin so much?" she asked.

"It's my magic," said Mae sadly. "Animals are attracted to my key chain. It helps them trust me when I first meet them."

Rachel's eyes opened very wide.

"Of course!" she said. "That's how the goblins kidnapped Pan Pan."

"We have to get the key chain back before we can rescue him," said Kirsty. "I have an idea. Mae, can you turn me into a goblin?"

"All right," said Mae, sounding a little nervous. "Get ready!"

She raised her wand, and Kirsty closed her eyes. She didn't like turning into a goblin. But she would do anything to help return Pan Pan to his mother.

A Daring Rescue

Kirsty felt her nose growing longer and her ears becoming pointy as her hair disappeared. Holding out her hands in front of her, she saw that they had turned green. Mae and Rachel, who were fluttering in the air beside her, suddenly looked very small.

"Wish me luck!" said Kirsty.

"Good luck!" whispered Mae and Rachel together.

Kirsty stepped out from behind the thicket of bamboo, and sat down beside the goblin with the big ears.

"Hello," she said, making her voice sound as squawky as she could. "Would you like me to hold that key chain while you rock the panda to sleep?"

"Don't be silly," said the goblin rudely. "This toy's the only thing keeping the panda with me. If you took the toy, he'd go to you instead."

"I didn't know that!" screeched a plump goblin.

He immediately snatched the magic key chain and Pan Pan woke up with a jump. Instantly, the little panda scampered after the special charm. But another goblin grabbed it, and Pan Pan changed direction. With a cry of

fury, the goblin with the big ears chased
after the others and seized the key chain.

Kirsty leaped up and followed the big-
eared goblin, trying to take the magic
key chain out of his hands. But then
she heard a whimpering noise. Poor
little Pan Pan was crying. He didn't
understand what was happening—he
just wanted his toy back.

Mae couldn't bear to see him crying.

"We have to stop this!" she said. She flew out from her hiding place, closely followed by Rachel.

"FAIRIES!" screeched the tallest goblin. "Get them! Trap them!"

Rachel zoomed toward the big-eared goblin, and Kirsty started jumping up and down.

"There's a fairy right behind you!" she yelled at the goblin. "Quick, throw the toy to me!"

The goblin hurled the key chain to Kirsty. Instantly, Pan Pan toddled over to her. She scooped him up in her arms and gave Rachel and Mae a beaming smile.

"We did it!" she said as they landed on her shoulders. "Pan Pan is safe."

"And so is my panda key chain," said Mae, her eyes sparkling with happiness.

Kirsty handed her the panda key chain, and it shrank to fairy-size. Pan Pan gave a sad squeak as Mae clipped the charm to her belt. Rachel fluttered down and stroked Pan Pan's wet little nose.

"Don't be sad," she said in a soft voice. "We're taking you home to your mother."

The goblins gaped at Kirsty in amazement. They still thought that she was one of them!

"What did you do that for?" yelled the tallest goblin. "Are you crazy? Jack Frost will be furious!"

With a wave of her wand, Mac
transformed Kirsty into a human again.
The goblins let out howls of rage.

"You tricky fairies!"

"Cheats! Cheats!"

"Give that panda back!"

The tallest goblin turned to the goblin
with big ears and stamped on his foot.

"This is all your fault!" he squawked.
"If we'd gone when I said we should,
we'd be at the Ice Castle by now!"

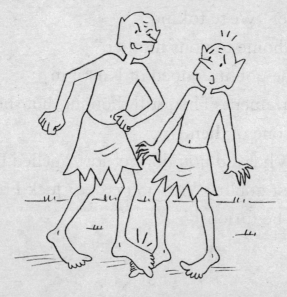

"What's Jack Frost going to say?" asked the plump goblin, his knees knocking together in fear.

"Maybe we should go into hiding," said the fourth goblin.

"Good idea!" said the tallest goblin. "Come on, let's run for it!"

The girls and Pan Pan watched as the goblins disappeared into the bamboo forest. Then Mae turned Rachel back to human-size.

"Can I hold Pan Pan?" Rachel asked at once.

Kirsty smiled and handed her the little panda. Just then, they heard running footsteps and the goblin with big ears came hurrying back out of the bamboo forest. Rachel held on tightly to Pan Pan. What was the goblin going to do?

A Panda
Present

The goblin stopped in front of Rachel
and looked embarrassed.

"I just wanted to say good-bye," he said
in a shy voice.

Rachel bent down and let him give
Pan Pan a tickle.

"Good-bye, little panda," he whispered.

Then he scurried away, and Rachel
lifted Pan Pan onto her shoulders.

"Pan Pan, you're so sweet that you even melted the heart of a goblin," said Kirsty with a laugh. "Come on, let's take you home."

Together, the girls and Mae made their way back through the crackling bamboo stems and the wet grass. They found Pan Pan's mother sheltered under the beautiful pagoda.

As soon as she saw them, his mother
gave a happy cry.

"Pan Pan!"

With a squeal of delight, Pan Pan
jumped off Rachel's shoulders and ran
into his mother's arms. As she showered
him in furry, snuffly kisses, she looked at
the girls with tears in her eyes.

"How can I ever thank you?" she
asked happily.

"There is one thing," said Kirsty with a little smile. "Would you let us take a picture of you and Pan Pan?"

A few minutes later, Rachel and Kirsty had some beautiful shots of Pan Pan and his mother.

"Now it's time for us to go home," said Rachel, looking at her watch. "We've got to meet Becky at the nature reserve!"

Mae gave each of the girls a kiss on the cheek.

"You've been wonderful," she said. "I couldn't have saved Pan Pan or my magic key chain without you. Thank you!"

"You're welcome," said Kirsty. "The Baby Animal Rescue Fairies can always count on our help."

"We're going to need it," said Mae. "There are still six magic key chains to find. But in the meantime, I'll send you back to Wild Woods Nature Reserve. Good-bye, girls!"

She waved her wand and Rachel and Kirsty felt themselves being lifted into the air. Warm rain sprinkled against their faces as Mae's fairy magic whisked them across the world. A few moments later, they were standing at the entrance to the nature reserve and Becky was hurrying toward them.

"There you are, girls!" she called. "I was beginning to wonder if you'd gotten lost! Did you have a good time?"

"Wonderful!" said Kirsty.

"Spectacular!" said Rachel with a big smile.

"That's great!" said Becky. "Now, I've got a job for you to do. We've cleared a space for some new trees, so I'd like you to plant the saplings."

Becky showed them where the young trees were lying on the ground beside a number of holes. She told them how to plant each one in its own hole. Just then, her radio crackled, and the girls heard a muffled voice.

"It sounds as if I'm needed up at the lake," Becky said. "Is it OK if I leave you to start planting?"

"Of course," replied Kirsty. "We'll come and find you when we're finished."

Becky hurried away, and Rachel picked up one of the saplings. She placed it in a hole, but it started to bend sideways.

"The trunks aren't sturdy enough to stand up by themselves," she said. "What are we going to do?"

As the girls stared at each other, there was a whooshing sound. A sprinkling of rainbow-colored fairy dust fell, and for a moment they thought they could smell the fresh, wet scent of the bamboo forest. Then they saw a bundle of bamboo poles on the ground between them, tied together with a thin rope made from grass.

"Look, there's a note," said Rachel.

Thank you!
With love from Mae and the pandas

At the bottom of the note were two panda paw prints from Pan Pan and his mother.

"What a lovely present," said Kirsty, sounding puzzled. "But how can bamboo help us?"

"I know!" said Rachel. "Remember how tall the bamboo grew in the forest? I bet the bamboo could help teach the saplings how to stand up straight!"

Eagerly, the girls set to work. Before very long, they had planted all the saplings, using the bamboo poles to support them. Becky came back just as they were finishing the last tree.

"That's fantastic, girls!" she exclaimed. "What a good way to use those bamboo poles, too. Where did you find them?"

"Oh, they were just lying around," said Rachel with a smile.

"Great work," said Becky. "I have a reward for you."

She pulled out a little box, which the girls could see was full of badges. Each badge had a different picture on it, and Becky sorted through them until she found what she was looking for.

"These badges show that you've helped to conserve trees," she said, handing one to each girl.

The badges had a picture of a tree on them. The girls pinned them on, feeling very proud.

"I can't wait to show Mom and Dad," said Kirsty.

Rachel looked at her watch.

"They'll be here to pick us up soon," she said. "Wow, today went by so fast!"

"That's good," said Becky. "I hope you've had fun."

"More fun than we could ever have imagined," Kirsty replied. "I can't wait to see what tomorrow will bring!"

As Becky turned away, the best friends smiled at each other and Rachel gave a wink. "More fairy adventures, I hope!"

THE BABY ANIMAL RESCUE FAIRIES

Rachel and Kirsty found Mae's
missing magic key chain.
Now it's time for them to help

Kitty
the Tiger Fairy!

Join their next adventure in this special
sneak peek . . .

Return to Wild Woods

"I can't wait to find out what we'll be doing today!" Rachel Walker exclaimed eagerly as she followed her best friend, Kirsty Tate, through Wild Woods Nature Reserve. "I hope we see lots of different animals."

It was summer vacation, and the girls' parents had arranged for them to spend a week as junior rangers at Kirsty's local

nature reserve. The reserve was a haven for all kinds of animals like hares, otters, and red squirrels.

"Look, Kirsty, there's Becky with the other junior rangers." Rachel pointed to the clearing ahead of them where a group of girls and boys were gathered around the head of the nature reserve. "I bet she has some interesting jobs for us!"

Becky was chatting with a couple of the junior rangers. She spotted the girls and waved to them.

"Everyone's here now, so good morning to you all," Becky announced with a huge smile. "I'm thrilled you're back for more important wildlife work here at Wild Woods Nature Reserve! Did you have a good time yesterday?"

"YES!" everyone shouted, full of excitement.

"Well, we have a very busy day ahead of us," she informed them. "I have a special job for you down at the stream. You can start off by getting yourselves dressed in *these*!" Becky pointed to a bunch of tall rubber boots piled on the grass beside her. Rachel and Kirsty lined up with the other junior rangers to grab a pair, and then they pulled on the rubber boots. The boots were so tall, they covered their legs all the way up to their thighs.

"I feel like Puss-in-Boots!" Kirsty said to Rachel with a grin.

Becky grabbed a rake that was leaning against a nearby tree and a net lying on

the grass. "Follow me, everyone," she called, walking off through the woods.

"I wonder why we're going to the stream," Rachel remarked as everyone followed Becky. "I hope we'll be able to do the special job, whatever it is."

"If we finish it, we might get another badge," Kirsty said hopefully. Becky had given the girls badges with a picture of a tree on them after they'd successfully planted some young saplings the day before. Rachel and Kirsty had proudly pinned the badges to their backpacks. "And maybe"—Kirsty lowered her voice so that no one else could hear—"our fairy friends will need our help again today, too!"

RAINBOW magic™

Which Magical Fairies Have You Met?

- ❏ The Rainbow Fairies
- ❏ The Weather Fairies
- ❏ The Jewel Fairies
- ❏ The Pet Fairies
- ❏ The Dance Fairies
- ❏ The Music Fairies
- ❏ The Sports Fairies
- ❏ The Party Fairies
- ❏ The Ocean Fairies
- ❏ The Night Fairies
- ❏ The Magical Animal Fairies
- ❏ The Princess Fairies
- ❏ The Superstar Fairies
- ❏ The Fashion Fairies
- ❏ The Sugar & Spice Fairies
- ❏ The Earth Fairies
- ❏ The Magical Crafts Fairies

■ SCHOLASTIC

Find all of your favorite fairy friends at
scholastic.com/rainbowmagic

RMFAIRY11

SPECIAL EDITION

Which Magical Fairies Have You Met?

3 stories in each one!

☐ Joy the Summer Vacation Fairy
☐ Holly the Christmas Fairy
☐ Kylie the Carnival Fairy
☐ Stella the Star Fairy
☐ Shannon the Ocean Fairy
☐ Trixie the Halloween Fairy
☐ Gabriella the Snow Kingdom Fairy
☐ Juliet the Valentine Fairy
☐ Mia the Bridesmaid Fairy
☐ Flora the Dress-Up Fairy
☐ Paige the Christmas Play Fairy
☐ Emma the Easter Fairy
☐ Cara the Camp Fairy
☐ Destiny the Rock Star Fairy
☐ Belle the Birthday Fairy
☐ Olympia the Games Fairy
☐ Selena the Sleepover Fairy
☐ Cheryl the Christmas Tree Fairy
☐ Florence the Friendship Fairy
☐ Lindsay the Luck Fairy
☐ Brianna the Tooth Fairy
☐ Autumn the Falling Leaves Fairy
☐ Keira the Movie Star Fairy
☐ Addison the April Fool's Day Fairy
☐ Bailey the Babysitter Fairy
☐ Natalie the Christmas Stocking Fairy
☐ Lila and Myla the Twins Fairies

■SCHOLASTIC

Find all of your favorite fairy friends at
scholastic.com/rainbowmagic

HIT entertainment

RMSPECIAL14